MW00744002

THE ADVENTURES

OF AUGUST WINTER

AND THE BLACKSTONE ACADEMY

Written And Illustrated By

C.S. ROBADUE

Welcome to the world of August Winter! I am so thrilled that you have found this book and can share in the adventure. It is intended to be the first of many; enjoy the ride, and thanks for checking it out!

- C.S. Robadue

WaveGarden Arts LLC

***

ISBN-10: 1505300770
ISBN-13: 978-1505300772

www.wavegardenarts.com

For My Parents
Who have always encouraged me to dream

THE ADVENTURES
OF AUGUST WINTER

AND THE BLACKSTONE ACADEMY

CHAPTER ONE

In many ways it appeared to be a typical summer day in the charming colonial city of Providence, Rhode Island. A soft wind in the air rustled the leaves on the trees in front of the domed RI State House, before continuing on its winding way towards downtown. The breeze swirled around the soaring façade of the art deco tower at the heart of the city, sending the wayward wind headed east over the Moshassuck River, towards College Hill. An old neighborhood, formerly known to locals as Prospect Hill, it boasted an eye-pleasing mixture of wrought iron and brickwork that framed the historic buildings, giving off a distinct feel that you were indeed in New England.

Downtown, on the border between the Financial and Jewelry districts, the well-worn city streets were lined with many shops, including a popular local convenience store. Inside, walking amidst the aisles filled with snacks, greeting cards, diapers, soda, and milk was a young man in his early teens wearing worn jeans and cowboy boots. Nicknamed JJ by his friends, not only for his striking resemblance to the famous outlaw Jesse James, but also for having the reputation of being able to steal anything without ever getting caught. With alert eyes he quietly tried to avoid the attention of the store clerk at the cash register, who only occasionally glanced around the store while he attended to other customers.

Largely distracted, the store's clerk was busy chatting up a woman in a blue dress in the checkout line. Sensing that the moment was right, JJ, as silently and stealthily as possible, stuffed an entire loaf of bread under his shirt and handfuls of candy into his pockets. No one seemed to notice. Having cased the establishment well, he knew he was operating in the blind spot of the security camera that was stuck in the upper corner of the store by the refrigerated goods.

His red and brown plaid shirt now stuffed full, he backed away from the shelves and carefully started to circle the long way around the perimeter of the store, toward the exit. Painstakingly, he attempted to remain hidden from view and to keep the sudden growth under his shirt unnoticed! He was nearly to the door, and sweet, sweet freedom, when something caught his eye…

It was the latest issue of his favorite magazine! Pausing for a second, he debated what to do. Imagining how impressed the other boys would be if he could break his own record and add it to the day's haul, he overrode his better judgment.

Snatching it, he jammed the magazine up under his shirt, which was now stretched out comically far. Turning, he was not able to complete a single step before disaster struck. The magazine had disrupted the balance of loot under his shirt and stuff was falling out left and right, crinkling loudly as it fell and hit the floor!

Panic-stricken, the young man didn't dare even look up. Knowing full well that he now had the clerk's complete attention!!

"Hey!" the clerk shouted angrily, not yet leaving his post behind the counter.

Grabbing up a bit of candy and the loaf of bread while leaving the rest, JJ took off like his pants were on fire, making for the store exit. Rushing by the front counter at high speed he cleared the doorway and took a sharp left hoping to quickly get out of sight.

"Oh no! Not today you don't!" shouted the clerk.

Leaping over the counter, he was immediately in hot pursuit of the shoplifter on foot. Leaving a line of customers confused and bewildered, while waiting to purchase their assorted goods.

Outside, the world seemed fresh and clear to JJ. The rhythmic clicking of his cowboy boots striking the concrete preceded him as he ran wildly. Racing down the sidewalk, he only occasionally looked back behind him to see if the store clerk was still on his tail. If the sound of the angry shouts and cursing were any indication, he hadn't lost him yet!

Slowed down by the busy midday foot-traffic filling the sidewalks, JJ forced himself to push onward, unceremoniously shoving people aside, as he tried to put more distance between himself and the erupting monster chasing at his heels!

"For the last time, stop, I said!!" yelled the clerk from several blocks back, while he too tried to fight his way through the crowds.

Pretending not to hear, JJ rushed across the street in front of the historic Providence Arcade building, his course now veering closer to the heart of the Financial district and the main Downtown plaza. He intended to lose himself in the throngs of people waiting at the bus station and around the edge of Burnside Park.

Doing his best to keep up, the clerk leaped out into the street himself, and barely avoided being struck by a small commercial truck, as he blindly bolted across the road after the young man.

Noontime in the heart of the city meant the plaza was teeming with loads of people getting picked up and dropped off at the bus terminal. Today was no exception; the scene was an absolute zoo. People blanketed the sidewalks and filled the park benches waiting for their scheduled buses.

In the distance, by City Hall, a silver charter bus was making its way through the fray, as it headed towards its destination on the East Side of the city. Passing the public transit buses, it picked up speed as it rounded the far corner of the plaza.

Walking casually along the sidewalk, immune to the chaos of his surroundings, was a very well-dressed man in a black suit with a visible crescent-shaped scar on his left hand. He was intently reading a newspaper article about a new art exhibit. Specifically for a traveling show of the Renaissance master Titian's work, that was to be displayed at the local art museum. It had captured his complete attention as he rounded the corner at the end of the block.

At the same moment, JJ gasped for breath, and hurtled out of the connecting alley out into the crowded walkway. Not looking, he plowed head first into the well-tailored man in black. It was a fantastic collision, with the last of the candy JJ was carrying going flying everywhere! The impact sent the two of them sprawling into the road directly in the path of the charter bus, the sad loaf of bread being flattened as they landed on the hard ground.

First came the flash of silver, then the searing sound of the bus's brakes being slammed, as the driver attempted desperately to stop the huge bus in time…

Flailing backwards in an instinctive reaction, JJ, helpless to the forces acting around him, watched with arms outstretched in defiance; as the bus came to a grinding halt mere centimeters from his face. Shocked and frozen, he strained his eyes to look up at the bus. The noontime sun blinded him as it reflected off the dark lifeless windows of the steel beast before him.

Unseen from the street below, cut off from the gasps and groans of horror reverberating through the crowd gathering outside, were the occupants of the bus. All of whom were children, that after the bus driver's evasive maneuvers were grasping their seats as if they were holding on for dear life!

Looking at JJ from behind the double-paned glass of the bus was the face of fourteen-year-old August Winter. Who hours ago, was thrilled at the prospect of his older brother letting him have the window seat on the long bus ride down to Providence, Rhode Island from Leverett, Massachusetts. His earnest face glued to the window in concern, his dark green collared shirt and uncomfortable dress shoes felt restrictive as his heart pounded and feet began to sweat.

Everything seemingly had stopped, as if waiting for someone to flip a switch and let the world breathe a collective sigh of relief. Staring into the eyes of a person who was at the edge of their very self, August could feel the panic and fear inside of JJ.

Already, the man in black was standing up and brushing himself off. Composed, he turned his attention to the young man who knocked him over and was still shaking on the ground. Grabbing the boy by his shirt, he hoisted him back up onto his feet and proceeded to unleash one heck of a strong stare down in his direction.

As if to snap the rest of the world back into motion, JJ was suddenly tackled from behind by the store clerk. Down again he went, as he was ripped out of the man-in-black's hands. This sparked a fierce argument between the well-dressed man and the clerk. Around them the ever-growing crowd of onlookers watched the scene unfold. No one seemed to know how to react, as if somehow they were all miles away, watching the events happen on the evening news, from the safety of their couches, instead of right before their eyes. Seeing that no one was hurt, and in an act of questionable ethics and decision making, the bus driver decided to get his rig out of there!

With a laborious sound from the engine, the bus shifted into gear as the traffic light down the street had turned from red to green. August stared after the scene as it shrank into the distance. No one said a word.

Moving right along, the charter bus passed over the river to College Hill and up Waterman Street as it headed towards the East Side and its destination. They passed by the Ivy League campus of Brown University, with all its brick and stone buildings that housed college students, classrooms, research labs, and libraries.

August took it all in, seeing it for the first time, making note of all the signs and populated walkways of Thayer Street. With its mix of lively shops, restaurants, and flocks of young people milling about before classes start. It was quite the sight to behold for a fellow coming from a small town such as himself.

He turned to look at his brother sitting next to

him. Unmoved by the sights outside the window, his brother sat, eyes closed, listening to music on his headphones, completely oblivious. He'd been half asleep the entire time, and had conveniently missed everything. Typical!

Tree-lined streets awaited the bus as it made a few turns and entered the residential part of the East Side. Large old Victorian homes, elaborate Tudors, sprawling Mediterranean residences, as well as other architecturally distinctive properties met the eye all along Blackstone Blvd. The manicured lawns and elaborate gardens of the rich all silently spoke to the work of the small army of landscapers that descend upon this community during normal business hours.

Through the rear-view mirror, the bus driver could see that August was completely enthralled with the sights outside the window.

"Is this your first year at the Academy?" he asked casually, half keeping his eyes on the road.

"Yes sir," August replied, no longer looking out the window.

"Ah. Well it's one of the oldest and highest-regarded preparatory schools in the entire country, with students hailing from all over the world. And since there is no cost to attend, admission is based entirely on merit alone. A rare thing indeed!" remarked the bus driver.

August responded by nodding his head in silent agreement, feeling the weight of all this new experience.

"Thus bringing together some of the most gifted young minds, regardless of class, wealth, or social status. As Blackstone Academy has always been supported entirely by its endowments and generous benefactors," continued the bus driver.

"I've never been to a boarding school before. But my parents made it clear that the decision was mine to make after I was selected to attend," said August.

"And a wise choice you made!" the bus driver said warmly.

While the old charter bus slowed to make a sharp turn, August's heart started to beat faster once again as he spotted the sign for the school. Weeks of anticipation were about to come to fruition, as he had arrived at his new scholarly home!

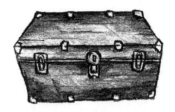

CHAPTER TWO

Entering the Blackstone Academy campus grounds, it was easy to recognize the markings of a school with a long-standing tradition. From its ivy-covered buildings to its old growth trees, the place lived and breathed history and distinction. Given the weathered and haggard look of the campus's well-worn structures, it was also clear that many were in dire need of attention and repair.

Slowing to a full stop at the edge of the large rectangular campus quad, the air brakes on the bus let out a loud hiss. Simultaneously, the bus driver swung open the charter's door in one smooth motion.

"Here we are, folks," wheezed the bus driver, as

if he too was letting out air.

Stretching his arms timidly, August held a very long blink before slowly opening his eyes. All right, he thought to himself, you can do this! Magically alert, his older brother Winston had already gotten up and taken down his personally monogrammed duffel bag from the overhead compartment.

"Good thing we were able to cram all of your stuff into that one old trunk, huh? It's quite a haul to the freshman dorms from here," remarked Winston.

"Really? Which one is it?" asked August, peering out the window. As there were a series of large stone brick dormitories surrounding the perimeter of the campus quad.

Pointing to a four-story brick building at the far end of the quad, Winston said, "Way over there. Come on, I'll show you."

Gathering up their stuff, the two boys exited the bus. It had been a fairly long ride and they were happy to move their legs once more. Outside the bus, there was a lineup of footlockers being arranged in no particular order on the lawn by the bus driver, as he cleared out the storage area of the old charter.

"I'll come back for my trunk later," said Winston, intent on helping his brother get settled in first.

The two of them took August's heavy dark blue footlocker, with its worn brass lock and tarnished trim, by the handles and started lugging it across campus towards the freshman dorm. Other upperclassman students had already arrived, and were playing an assortment of lawn games on the large campus green around them. Bocce, badminton, croquet, pretty much all the sort of games whose names sounded like they could accidentally be confused with items on a trendy cafe's breakfast menu were being played. There wasn't a single adult in sight.

Reaching the wide steps to the freshman dorm, the two brothers hoisted the weight of the footlocker up the cement steps. A small group of students wearing white lab coats were working just beyond the steps on something clearly scientific. On closer inspection, one would see that the embroidered words 'Rocket Club' could readily be made out on the backs of their lab coats. All of these rocket-scientists-in-the-making were circling what appeared to be a very elaborate and high-tech bottle rocket construct that was preparing for launch!

Pushing open the massively heavy old wooden doors of the freshman dorm, August and Winston entered into a grand lobby with high ceilings. Dark wainscoting and a rich array of the school's colors of green and gold greeted the brothers' eyes. Stepping forward, the wide-plank oak floors creaked and groaned as they lumbered across the room in search of the main stairs. The air was a bit musty, as it often could be in old buildings. August took in his new surroundings, noting the elaborate details and coloring in the large tapestry covering the ground floor lobby's wall. Motioning with a half-nod of his head, Winston directed them both towards a large wooden staircase. They slowly began to climb.

At the top of the stairwell, on the fourth floor, the dusty landing was the first to hear the heavy echoing footsteps of August and Winston's arrival at their destination. Together they plodded up the final few steps, dragging the footlocker behind them.

"Had to get assigned a room on the top floor, huh?" Winston asked rhetorically.

Glancing over the crumpled sheet of paper he was carrying in his hand, August double-checked his room assignment.

"Says here I'm in room 417," replied August, with a cautious but excited tone to his voice.

Wiping the perspiration off his brow, Winston was quick to remember his first days as a freshman, only two short years ago.

"Ah, right, should be just over here then. Follow

me," he called out as he headed down the hallway.

By now, other freshmen students had taken to the corridors wearing their monogrammed school blazers. All of them trying to find exotic destinations, like the fourth floor washroom! Trudging onward over the well-worn carpeting that had seen decades of fourteen-year-olds' foot traffic, the brothers were quick to arrive at Room 417. Finding the door open, August and Winston paused, then leaned their heads into the room.

"Knock, knock," said Winston sarcastically as he rapped his knuckles against the door's tired wooden trim.

"Who's there?" replied a voice from somewhere within the room.

"August," said August with a quizzical sound to his words.

"August who?" countered the mystery voice.

"August Winter... uh, your roommate?" he said, totally befuddled.

Laughing to himself, August's new roommate swung around from his hiding place behind his computer chair and faced August and his brother.

Grant was an easygoing guy and was clearly enjoying this play on the oldest of joke formulas.

"Right, right, good to meet you! My name's Grant, and I hope you don't mind. I made myself at home and have chosen this side of the room." With his laptop already set up, a scattering of personal items gracing the floor, and a mound of clothes covering one of the dressers, it was clear Grant had claimed the right half of the room.

"No problem at all," said August.

Utilizing the pause in conversation, August took a moment to look around at his new surroundings. It was a small room, with one large window looking out onto the quad and the unkempt gardens in front of the building. The window let enough light in to make the space feel comfortable and inviting. There was a pair of tiny closets opposite one another by the doorway. Plus dressers for each of them, as well as two modest twin beds that lined either wall, creating a long corridor through the room. With desks for both August and Grant on either side of the window at the far end of the room.

"Care for a pretzel?" asked Grant as he extended the freshly opened bag of pretzel sticks that he'd been munching on in August's direction.

"Yeah, thanks!" said August, already warming to his new environment.

Attempting to appear interested in the banter, August's brother Winston couldn't hide a bored look on his face and was itching for a reason to take off.

Pretending to check the time on a watch that he didn't have on his wrist, Winston spoke up.

"So you two are all settled in? Great! Guess I'll be off then. Now remember, it's vital that you…"

Cut off mid-sentence by the ringing of the cell phone from within his own pocket, Winston stopped his story to answer it.

"Excuse me. Have to take this."

Winston turned around and faced the hallway. Both Grant and August looked at each other and then back at Winston, then back at each other, then back at Winston again. Wondering what the heck he was about to reveal to them before his phone rang??

"Uh-huh, yup, right, okay, sure, you got it, uh-huh," mumbled Winston into the phone. Ending his call as abruptly as he had answered it, he put the phone back into his pocket. The room was now silent and full of suspense wondering what Winston would say!

"Gotta run, was glad to help, you guys have a great year. Later!"

And with that, he was off. Disappeared out the door, down the stairs, through the lobby, and halfway across the quad before August and Grant could make heads or tails of the situation. Bewildered, they continued munching on pretzels.

"Your brother seems nice enough, what year is he here?" wondered Grant aloud.

"He's a junior, and has already informed me that he isn't going to hold my hand since he didn't have anyone here to show him the ropes either. And that, ultimately, he was doing me a big favor, haha," said August.

"Very thoughtful of him, haha," returned Grant unable to hold in his laughter any longer.

"Yeah, I thought so too!" answered August, the two of them laughing and carrying on.

Suddenly, an explosion rocked the building, with purple smoke filling the hallway and beginning to permeate the entrance into their room! Could this have been what August's brother was going to warn them about??!?

Frightened, Grant blurted out, "Uh, is it just me or are you seeing this too??! And tell me I'm not the only one who heard that loud boom??"

Ready to dive under his bed at any second, Grant was clearly rattled.

"Glad you said it man, 'cause something is definitely up!" stammered August, ready to do the same.

His eyes turned to the door, August contemplated kicking off an investigation of what was going on!

Before even getting the chance they were immediately surprised by a visitor! As out of the thick heavy purple fog, a head of wild shaggy blonde hair seemed to have materialized.

The small face peering around the doorway and through the thick fog identified himself as Shelby from next door. He was wearing an impressive set of glasses, over top of which he had added a pair of safety goggles intertwined with his feisty collection of tangled hair.

"I did it!! Can you believe it?!?!" said Shelby, hardly able to contain his excitement long enough to enunciate his words.

Pausing, Grant and August didn't know what to say, still dazed by the entire chain of events taking place around them.

August recovered first and assessed the situation. Smiling, August said, "Does seem to have all the earmarks of a momentous occasion!"

"You said it! And I had hoped the formula was correct this time, as my prior attempts have not ended well…" said Shelby, shaking his head wistfully.

"Not at all… But!! We lucked out this time, and oh, the sweetness of success!"

Taking out a clipboard and pen, Shelby was soon lost writing down his observations and thoughts on his

latest chemistry breakthrough! Stopping only to chew the end of the pen and drum it against the frame of his glasses, before diving back into his findings.

Waving his hands through the purple fog that had taken over his side of the room, Grant asked the question that would be the first thing on nearly any astute (or otherwise!) observer's mind.

"Uh, dare I ask what exactly the breakthrough was, or is?" he sputtered.

"Oh, right, of course!" returned Shelby, looking up from his paper full of scribbles. Lowering his voice, he leaned in as if to tell them both a diabolical secret. "Between us, I figured out a formula for making... glow-in-the-dark toothpaste!!" whispered Shelby.

"That's brilliant!" declared an impressed August, shaking Shelby's hand in congratulations.

Smiling triumphantly, Shelby stood back and took a moment to take in the admiration that was clearly not a normal reaction he was used to receiving for his scientific work.

Grant was less than immediately convinced of the brilliance of this 'breakthrough'.

"Is it safe? For people I mean?" he asked.

"Safe? Absolutely, this first batch is spearmint, too!" said Shelby.

"Amazing…think of how awesome it would be when you're out camping or something," pointed out August.

"Yeah! The only thing…" Shelby paused and tilted his head as if he was listening to something far off in the distance.

Uncomfortable with the silence, Grant nervously asked, "What??!!"

Shelby rapped the pen cap against his head and scratched behind his ear as if trying to buy time to come up with the right words.

"Well…. The purple gas by-product is a trifle bit unstable. Haven't quite figured that part out yet, rather a nuisance really." With a calculated nod, Shelby looked rather grave for a moment.

"How unstable?" asked August, reading into the situation, his brow raised in concern.

"Hmm, it has a nasty habit of being rather explosive," said Shelby nonchalantly.

"Explosive!!" exclaimed August.

Un-phased, Shelby replied, "Yes, but only if given the proper spark, and what are the chances of that? We're quite safe in here, I suspect."

Meanwhile, outside by the front steps, a certain club had finished preparations for a certain launch of a certain rocket!! They had all donned safety goggles and had given the rocket a wide berth in anticipation of ignition. The head of the club had a detonator in hand that was attached by wire to the base of the rocket. She began a countdown.

"Three…. Two…. One…. Lift off!!!!" At that moment, she pressed down on the plunger and the rocket flew into action! The whole group of students let out a loud cheer as their creation zoomed upward to meet the sky head-on.

Mere seconds after takeoff, tragedy struck! One of the fins at the base of the rocket cracked, flapped, and fell off!! Leaving the rocket lopsided and spinning wildly. It veered dramatically off course and began doing curlycues in the air over the quad, going around trees, students, and buildings, until it headed straight towards the freshman student dorm!

Unaware of what, at that very moment, was happening out on the quad, August, Grant, and Shelby remained standing in the dorm room discussing this scientific breakthrough. The purple fog still lingered thick in the air.

"That is true, what are the chances…" added Grant sounding more relieved.

Turning to his left, a flicker of motion outside the

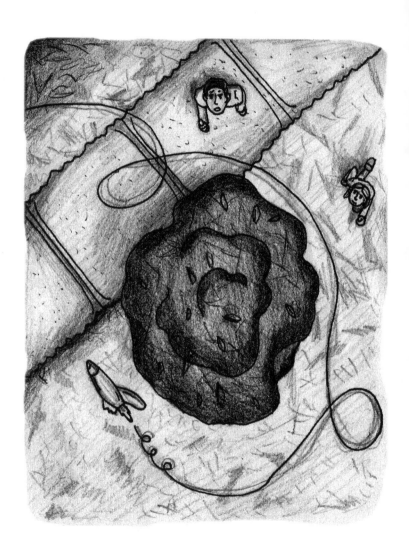

window caught August's attention. Tilting his head, he tried to get a better look out the window, as there was a tree branch partially blocking the view.

What he saw astonished him, as a wildly out of control rocket was careening straight for their dorm room window! It was getting bigger and bigger by the second as it came closer and closer into view. Noticing that something had locked August's attention, both Grant and Shelby turned to look out the window too.

"Oh boy..." said August. All their heads now focused on the window, the three of them let out a loud collective "Ahhhhh!!!!!!!"

Shattering the small panes of glass in the process, the rocket flew through the fourth floor window of August and Grant's dorm room. An enormous, loud vhooooom could be heard all across campus as the spark of the rocket propulsion triggered the reactive quality of the purple fog, and vwoooooommmp, a huge purple cloud/explosion enveloped the room.

Caught off guard by the sudden crash landing in their midst, the three boys were knocked off their feet and laid flat out in various contorted forms of general disarray on the floor! Dazed, the guys tried to gather their wits and figure out what the heck had just happened!

All three were completely unharmed by the surprise attack. Though the sight of all their hair standing on end, as if they had just put their fingers in an electrical socket, spoke volumes that this was no ordinary snapshot of scholarly life! No longer was there a purple cloud lingering in the air, instead there was a dense purple residue peppered all over the walls, the furniture, the floor, and, not to be outdone, the boys' faces!

"Extraordinary!" marveled Shelby.

Looking at each other, and the state of the room, both August and Grant laughed to the point of tears, as each had a look that could only be described as a big frightful purple shambles!

"Haha, August, I'd like you to officially meet our neighbor, Shelby. Bit of a chemistry enthusiast, you might say!" laughed Grant.

Extending his hand, August happily shook Shelby's hand. It was quite the sight, considering that both boys were an electrified purple mess.

"Pleasure to meet you, August!" said Shelby.

"Likewise! That was some crazy display, I can tell it's going to be an interesting year already!" said August smiling widely.

CHAPTER THREE

Daylight had arrived on the East Side and activity on campus had already begun. It was a perfect picturesque September morning with blue skies and a slight breeze creating that familiar yet wonderful rushing sound of the leaves upon the trees. The hands of the large clock at the peak of the Administration building by the top of the quad were pointing towards eight o'clock, while the deep bass tones of the clock's chimes rumbled across the lawn, as if calling the day to order in a courtroom, yet awaiting no reply.

It was the first day of classes at Blackstone Academy and dozens of students with backpacks in tow filed out of their dorms and headed off to the different academic buildings on campus. Despite the early hour, there was still a sense of excitement amongst the students as old friends were reunited, while new ones met for the first time. Some might call it the calm before the storm. Being one of those fleeting moments where homework, lab reports, and term papers were still concepts lost in the abstraction of the future.

Headmaster Humboldt, who had led the school for nearly thirty years, was out and about on his bicycle. Riding around campus, he made sure that everything was taking place smoothly, as it should be. Most people would describe him as a tall, lanky gentleman in his seventies with a fantastic white beard and that certain sense of worldly presence that had seen it all before. Barking the occasional directive, he was clearly pleased with how well everything was running on this particular morning.

Across campus, standing under an oak tree, two students were going over their schedules line by line, cross-checking them with their crumpled map from the back of a campus brochure. It was of course, August and Grant!

"We're definitely lost, no two ways about it," said Grant as he thrust his hands deeper into his pockets.

"Yeah, I could have sworn that last turn was the

one we needed to make. But I'm not seeing anything familiar. Should we randomly try one of these buildings and see if we hit upon the right one?" suggested August.

"Guess so. First though, which way is north from here?" asked Grant, his eyes still glued to the sad looking map in his hands.

"North, north, uh, if we flip this around, there, that way is north and we're right here," said August.

He pointed to a spot on the map showing that they had walked to the very limits of the area displayed, and were virtually off campus grounds and headed in the direction of Downtown Providence!

"Schedule says we need to be in Room 212 of Columbus Hall for our history class, which starts in, oh, six minutes!" croaked Grant, who was getting more anxious by the second.

As the two boys were thinking, Headmaster Humboldt spotted them in the distance and immediately keyed in on the situation. Biking over, the sound of his bicycle's squeaky brakes alerted the boys to his arrival.

"Okay, so listen; the way this works is that you, the students," pointing at August and Grant, "Make sure you get to the location specified on that sheet of paper at the time designated, it's that simple. Any questions? Better ask them now. As your education is only going to get more challenging from here, I assure you, so don't expect anyone to hold your hand," grumbled Headmaster Humboldt.

Frozen, Grant and August tried to nod their heads, but remained motionless, like squirrels caught away from a tree to climb. Frightened looks etched onto their faces in response to the bold execution of adult authority displayed before them. After several seconds of silence, a mental thawing occurred.

"Yes sir, of course, sir. But could we trouble you to point us in the direction of…" checking his schedule. "Columbus Hall?" croaked August quietly.

The headmaster repressed a warm smile, as he leaned back, cleared his throat and adjusted his glasses to hide his amusement.

"Columbus Hall, good starting point, lots to be learned in the annals of history," said Headmaster Humboldt. Nodding his head in agreement with his own words, the headmaster paused. The guys stood fixed in place, and waited for the directions as they were aware that time was running short for them to make it to their very first class on time.

"Turn yourselves around, head back the way you came, to the campus quad. Look for the building with the ramparts on top of it, and that's your destination," said

Headmaster Humboldt with purpose.

Craning their heads to look behind them, August and Grant tried to recall visually the building that Headmaster Humboldt was referring to.

"So, what's the hold up, why all this standing around acting useless? Get yourselves moving!" shouted Headmaster Humboldt.

As if struck by lightning, they jumped into action and scrambled off towards the center of campus at high speed. Left behind, Headmaster Humboldt chuckled to himself, as he was quite certain he had made a strong impression on this pair of freshman students.

Very few students remained on the quad, but those who did were like August and Grant, sprinting rapidly across the grass, intent to get to their classes on time. Moving as fast as their legs would carry them, the guys flew up the steps of Columbus Hall and burst through the main doors. Still more steps awaited them as they zipped up the stairs to the next level in search of Room 212. Reaching the second floor, they spilled out onto the tiled floor of the hallway, sliding as they went. Spotting the door for 221, they were so close now, with just mere seconds remaining!

Running down the hall it was like a countdown, going from room to room, 218, 216, 214 and so on!

Skidding to a stop as they reached 212, they tore open the door just as the final bell rang. They'd made it! All the other students had already taken their seats and every face in the room was fixed on the two latest arrivals. At the front of the classroom, the teacher, Mr. Eastley, waved for them to come in. He was a jovial and energetic man in his late sixties, with blondish white hair and a fantastically impressive full mustache.

"Welcome, fellows, you're just in time! Find a comfortable seat, for we are about to begin our journey back in time," rattled Mr. Eastley from his vantage point by the blackboard.

It was clear that Mr. Eastley was not your typical run-of-the-mill teacher and one shouldn't be too certain of what to expect from his class!

Moving around the outer reaches of the room, August and Grant still felt as if all eyes were on them. It was a smallish classroom and the only open seats were in the first row. 'Super', August thought to himself, no way to keep a low profile when we're front and center.

Looking about his surroundings, he saw that the classroom itself was filled with ancient objects and shelves loaded to the gills with books, while a large wall of tall glass windows invited the eye to wander. Uniform rows of desks running front-to-back inhabited the rest of the room.

Everyone was now seated, their notebooks out instinctively, as if the behavior had been engrained in their DNA from birth. Mr. Eastley began his lecture on the subject at hand, Western Civilization.

"Western Civilization, the traditions of Greece, Rome, medieval times, kings, conquerors, the rise of mighty empires, it is all here, under one very, very large umbrella of thoughts and ideas," said Mr. Eastley.

"Reminds me of the time I took my entire family on a daring trip to Devonshire. In England, you know. Wonderful excursion into the old world, where we would wake up at dawn's first light and hike for miles in the countryside. Across the moors, taking in the most delightful fresh air. One time we even came across Lord Cavendash himself with one of his premiere hunting hounds, on the trail of goodness knows what, capital fellow," continued Mr. Eastley, already off topic, in mid-semester form.

Taking down a few notes here and there, Grant glanced across the aisle from him. Sitting next to him was a lovely Asian girl who was writing in her notebook while listening to the lecture. She had definitely caught his attention as he watched her with a lot more interest than he had been paying to the history lesson! Her notebook had 'Property of Kasia' written on it in glossy markers. Noticing that she had an audience, Kasia stopped and looked over at Grant. He didn't even notice at first, so lost in his own day-dreaming.

Quietly tearing off a small piece of paper from her notebook, she scribbled down a note. All the while, Mr. Eastley continued on with his lesson, writing on the board with his back to the class. Crumpling up the note she tossed it at Grant, who had finally recognized that his attention had not gone unnoticed. His brilliant defense was to pretend to be really focused on his textbook and to avoid eye contact with Kasia at all costs! The paper note ricocheted off his desk, onto his shoulder, before bouncing to the classroom floor below. Panicked, he alertly snatched it up. Unfolding it, he read the note to himself; it read, 'Can I help you with something??!'

Suddenly massively embarrassed, he felt totally busted, his pulse already beginning to race. Grant wracked his brain for something impossibly brilliant to write back. Nervously, he flipped over the note and tried to think of a clever reply.

To himself, 'Come on, think, Grant!!' Left with only his thoughts and no one to confer with, he turned in his reply. Folding up the scribbled note, while carefully watching for any movement from the teacher, Grant

lofted the note back in Kasia's direction.

Uncrumpling the note, she read it over and then shot Grant a confused and somewhat perturbed look. Then she gave her attention back to the lesson at hand as the lecture continued with more insightful European tales. Disappointed, Grant sulked, knowing he had made a lousy first impression. Theatrically, he mocked hitting his head on the desk. August saw his friend acting distressed and leaned over to say something.

"You alright??" whispered August. Unable to look him in the face, Grant continued to mope.

CHAPTER FOUR

Blackstone Academy was well-known for its historic campus, though it was clear to even the untrained eye that not every building there was in the best of condition. The great hall for dining was a definite exception, with its tall cathedral ceiling and intricate stonework speaking loudly of both the school's proud past and contemporary greatness. High above in the rafters, the large open area over the cafeteria was like a huge vacuum for ponderous thoughts as well as the smells of last week's chili and the lingering aroma of steamed cabbage.

Food at the academy was very traditional, not simply in presentation, but also in ingredients. Dishes based on a limited number of time-tested flavors and menu favorites were hallmarks of the meals. All balanced perfectly for a very wholesome, energizing diet. You'd have your vegetable, starch, protein, and choice of beverage. Yet the real culinary magic was in the desserts, as they had fantastic selections to choose from. On this particular day the menu had a lineup of beets, rice, grilled chicken, and string beans with a hint of garlic, of course! With all that healthy stuff gloriously followed by a delightful lemon meringue pie!

Sitting across from each other at one of the long wooden tables off the central corridor of the hall, August and Grant discussed the morning's events.

"'No, but could I help you with something?' That's what you said, really??? For real, man??" asked August incredulously, speaking to Grant's, uh, rather not so spectacularly worded note.

As if trying to hide from the world, Grant had his arms covering his face, his shoulders slouched.

"Gahhhhh, I know. It always seems to break that way for me. The opportunity presents itself and then, blam, just like that I figure out a way to make it awkward. Brilliantly, too, what a gift!" said Grant with a look of complete dejection on his face.

"It's all a mystery to me too, might as well be

like this beet here," said August in an effort to make Grant feel better. He took one of the beets off his plate with his fork and studied it intently.

"Haha, what? Can't say I'm following you on this one!" replied Grant.

"Well, I mean, we all have a sense for what we expect of things. Like this beet, you might think you know what it is going to taste like, heck, it could even be your favorite food!" said August.

"Uh, it's not," snorted Grant.

"Well, whatever, the point is that just by looking at it, we make assumptions about what it is going to taste like, how it will smell, what it will feel like, etc. But until we get there, we have no idea. Could be bitter, overcooked, stale, rotten, pickled, you name it! That element of unpredictability, that's life," said August.

Clearly not convinced, Grant continued eating and stabbed at his string beans with a fork.

"Guess I'll play it safe and stick with the green beans then, haha."

"Suit yourself! Hey, which class do we have next?" asked August.

Rustling through a disorganized stack of papers in his backpack, Grant soon had the answer.

"Schedule says… next up is Geometry, and I

think it wouldn't be the worst idea in the world for us to get over there slightly early. As we wouldn't want to get a bad reputation in the teachers' lounge, not on the first day, anyways!" joked Grant.

"Not a problem, in fact I'm pretty sure I actually even know which building it's in," pointed out August.

"Well then, I gotta like our chances, haha," said Grant with a laugh.

As the post-lunch carbohydrate coma set in for all the students, everyone in the geometry class struggled to stay awake. It was not made any easier by the monotone voice of the teacher discussing angle-side-angle formulas, and referencing smudged chalk diagrams on the blackboard. Sunlight was streaming in the third floor Geometry classroom from the wall of west-facing windows. August was sitting quietly towards the back of the classroom, as he and Grant made it much earlier to this class!

Looking out the window, August couldn't help but daydream a little. Such a beautiful day out, it seemed a crime to be indoors. Never easy to transition from the freedom and long days of summer, to being confined to a classroom, while the official seasonal calendar still reads summer! Outside the window, August could see that there wasn't much activity on the quad right now.

Occasionally, a bird would fly by the window, but it was a cardinal that was the first to stop. It perched happily on the ledge outside, mere feet from August's desk. Tilting its head and seemingly looking directly back at him, it almost seemed like he, too, was wondering what a fourteen-year-old boy was doing trapped behind glass on such a nice summer day!

By the front gate to the school, August glimpsed an old light-blue work van driving past. The sort of van favored by plumbers and high school garage bands. Slumped back in his chair, he saw that everyone else had opened up their textbooks. He did the same and flipped through the pages until he reached the correct section.

***

Across town at that moment, a finely tailored man in a dark suit, his hair slicked back, and wearing designer sunglasses stood leaned up against the iron railing of a private Benefit Street residence. On the other side of the street, across from this posh address was the entrance to Providence's premiere art museum.

The brick sidewalks of Benefit Street were still active with foot traffic as it was a perfect afternoon for a stroll through the city. Not to be outdone architecturally by its neighbors, the museum itself was housed in a fantastic old brick building with a large glass entryway. The walk up to the museum, highlighted with some sculptural work and discreet signage, pointed guests in the right direction.

Staying largely motionless and sipping on a designer cup of coffee, the Italian gentleman watched the scene. A familiar blue van drove by and stopped at the traffic light at the end of the block. The name 'Butternut Painting' was written in large lettering on the side of the van. It rumbled to a stop before heading straight and out of sight.

***

Meanwhile, downtown in the high rent district, the mid-day sun was reflecting brightly off the shiny exterior of a commercial real estate high rise. On the 14th floor of this exclusive Exchange Street address was, to the uninitiated, the office of Lexi Donovan, owner and signature realtor for Lexi Donovan Realty. They handled a fair portion of Rhode Island's most elite listings from the East Side, Newport, and Narragansett. The office was the epitome of chic and sleek interior design. Minimalist furniture was the rule and everything was clean and streamlined. Save for the paintings on the walls, the rest of the environment was completely white.

Above the front reception desk, in icy silver lettering, the Lexi Donovan name was prominently displayed. Running the desk was Charline March, whose patience, cool temper, and poise were on par with any of the world's Zen masters. She was fielding calls and there were several clients waiting in the lobby. Picking up the phone, she answered in her delightful British accent.

"Good afternoon, Lexi Donovan's office, yes, certainly, please hold." Setting the phone down, she buzzed Lexi's office where Ms. Donovan was working, not twenty paces away.

It was clear that Lexi was in deep thought and grappling with something on her mind. She sighed as the phone on her desk beeped and broke her train of thought.

"Yes Charline? Is it the counter for the property on Bellevue?" asked Lexi passively.

"I'm afraid not Ms. Donovan, no word from their agent yet. This rather is a personal call, from a Mr. Lewis," that name bringing to mind instant recognition.

"Sigh, what's this, the third time he's called this week alone?" asked Lexi.

"Fourth, miss, he is rather persistent," answered Charline.

"You go out one lousy time to dinner with a guy and then they won't give you a moments peace! Uh, I don't know... tell him, tell him I'm in a meeting. Tell him I moved to Brazil, anything!" exclaimed Lexi.

"Understood, I will take care of it, and the Carters are here for their three-thirty appointment. And looking into exploring all their downtown Providence living options," said Charline.

"Very good, send them in at once," said Lexi.

Spinning slightly in her chair, Lexi looked at the beautiful collection of artwork that adorned the walls of her office. This was what kept her going, the truth and beauty found in paintings. Nothing had been able to equal it in her life. Stopped by her reflection in the small mirror on her desk, she let the strain in her life show in her expression.

"Ugh, I feel like death warmed over. If only I could figure 'this' out; time is running short. And another all night strategy session might be the end of me!"

At that moment, a quiet knock on the door let her know that the Carters were eager for her attention and that it was time to switch proverbial hats. Standing with them, and handling the introductions, was her assistant.

"Ms. Donovan, the Carters, Floyd and Erma," said Charline, in her charming accent.

Doing a complete emotional 180 in less than a nanosecond, Lexi sprung into life and was every inch the fantastic businesswoman she's so well known for being, as she lit up the room with her magnetic smile.

"Welcome, come in, come in, please have a seat. Make yourself at home, oh, your clutch, yes, put it anywhere. We need room to think big, because I can tell that the daring vision you have for your home living environment is not by any means ordinary!" announced Lexi.

It was immediately clear from the wide grins on her clients' faces that Lexi had already won the Carters over. And, as soon as anything, they would be opening up their checkbook and happily writing a figure with more zeroes on the end of it than they had ever intended on spending!

CHAPTER FIVE

All was quiet on the Blackstone Academy campus. In the distance, the rush of cars on Interstate 195 sounded more like the ocean than a major US highway, and on campus it was the peaceful chirping of crickets that was the highlight of the evening, with its soothing refrain. All the campus walkways were lit up by lamplight, and the open entrance to the freshman dorm had a warm and inviting quality to it, like that of a hearth in wintertime. Shadows moving about the dorm room windows showed that the first-years were very much still awake!

Going hand-in-hand with the first day of school had come the first night of homework. For August, that included assignments from all his core courses. Trying not to get overwhelmed by the avalanche of assignments, he paced himself and proceeded methodically with the math homework that had dominated his attention for the last half hour.

Trunks largely emptied and unpacked during the afternoon, the boys' dorm room was looking very much established, with most of their clothes hung neatly in the closet (except for a few that had already managed to miss the hamper and find their places happily in a heap on the floor). August had his desk set up, with a tall stack of textbooks dominating the landscape, his laptop flipped open, ready to be put to use. Grant's desk looked more like NASA command central than the workspace of a fourteen-year-old. He had three linked monitors, a tablet, keyboard, massive wireless headphones, and yes, even a fourth screen, in the form of a laptop, perched at the end of his bed.

Working alone in the room, August was nearly finished with his geometry assignment when a jarring thud at the door let him know that Grant had returned from his errands. Cautiously, Grant was trying to safely navigate the narrow entryway of their room with an enormous shipping box grasped tightly in his mitts.

"Got the last of the stuff that my parents mailed

up to me from DC. Really hope they didn't forget anything!" wheezed a winded Grant.

Setting down the large cardboard box he was carrying, Grant started emptying the contents onto the floor. Inside, it was absolutely teeming with cables, videogame controllers, classic game systems, and yet another screen, this time a TV!

Surveying his desk, he saw that space was becoming an increasingly rare commodity. Grant honed in on the somewhat, kinda, sorta, empty top to one of the clothes dressers. Going over to it, he pushed aside the stacked t-shirts he had there, and set down the TV.

"I have all the best classic games, so we're in good shape man," said Grant proudly, as he pulled out stack after stack of games from what seemed to be a bottomless pit of a box.

"Wow, you weren't kidding, that certainly beats working on this homework, I'm spent. Was thinking we should explore the city a bit this coming weekend, checkout more of College Hill," August said, closing his geometry textbook.

By the dresser, half of the contents of Grant's delivery were already all over the floor, in a tangled mess of wires, controllers, and remotes. The number of extension cords and power cables he had plugged into one outlet via a surge protector was comical.

"Yeah, man, definitely," replied Grant. "Now, if only I can figure out where to plug all of this in. Okay, I think I got it."

Plugging in the last power cord from his impressive collection of electronic wired gadgets, Grant had a satisfied look on his face.

"Alright, let's fire one of these systems up and see what you got, August!" he said.

"Grant, the uh, power setup there looks a little overtaxed..." warned August, as Grant continued to try and coax the power supply to fit into the lone wall outlet in that corner of the room.

Glancing over at the power outlet that had about a million cords attached to it, Grant paused.

"Huh? Oh, well, maybe, but I'm sure the school has an updated electrical system; you'd think so, right??" he said.

Shrugging his shoulders in response, August made a blank expression on his face. Neither of them knew one way or another definitively what was going to happen. Grant proceeded as planned, turning on the TV and pressing the power button on the first game system; they held their breath and waited!

Right away, the game booted up, and a familiar

friendly game character icon and title screen appeared, with an accompanying nostalgically themed jingle.

"Sweet! Ha-hah!" yelled Grant in satisfaction. The two friends exchanged high-fives, and were psyched to begin playing.

"I never doubted it for a second!" laughed August.

"Oh yeah, right, haha. I told you it'd work!" Grant boasted. No sooner had he gotten the words out of his mouth when, fwwwoooop, all the lights in the entire dorm went completely out!!

Total darkness had taken hold of the first years' dorm! Every other student who had been working at computers, reading for class, and finishing homework was silent in shock. Everything had gone out in the boys' dorm room, and they were sitting in pitch black in front of Grant's impressive array of screens and monitors. There was really nothing else to say other than...

"Oh... crap!" blurted out Grant quietly.

From beyond the walls of their room, they began to hear shouts from disgruntled freshmen as a wave of frustration swept over the building amongst the students who had lost unsaved homework assignments, network connections, and the lights in their rooms. Not all the cries were negative, there was one solitary voice in the mix that was yelling out of happiness! Seconds later it was followed by an enthusiastic knocking at their door. Who could it be?? And why???

"Guys, guys, guess what, it works, it really works!!" said Shelby. Letting himself in the room, the noise of their exuberant young chemist neighbor couldn't be contained.

"What's that, Shelby?" asked August.

"See, look, my glow in the dark toothpaste, it is a success!" beamed Shelby. And, as he opened his mouth, they could clearly see the glow from his teeth. While he waved the toothbrush in his hand around like a magic wand, it illuminated the room. What stood out most though in the darkness were without question his pearly white teeth, like a smiling beacon in the night.

"I was brushing my teeth over in our floor's bathroom, when wham, ALL the lights go out. Whole building must have lost power, but I thought it was someone playing a prank on me, initially. Anyways, the test sample works, what do you think, guys, is it great or what??!" Shelby asked with his enormous smile shining brightly.

Still reeling from the events that had just gone down, August was trying to make his way across the room to his bed. His legs tangled in videogame cords as he reached out with his hands trying to guide himself in the darkness.

"Congratulations, Shelby, and I should think you probably could have about 250 or so dorm residents as customers, come, oh, tomorrow!" said August as he scrambled over a mass of laundry.

"Gah, this is great, just great," groaned Grant in the darkness.

"Isn't it though; thanks, fellas, I knew you'd understand! Whoa, look at the time; I've got to go call my father with the good news. See ya!" said Shelby, and with that he took off out the door into the deep abyss of the darkened hallway.

"See ya, Shelby," called out Grant, "And let's hope no one finds out that it was my fault!" he whispered to August.

CHAPTER SIX

After an eventful night of accidentally sabotaging the freshman dorm's electrical system, August and Grant set out for class the following morning. The two friends leaped up the steps of the entryway to the Tesla Science Center, named after the brilliant engineer and inventor Nikola Tesla, who was famous for his work with electricity and alternating current induction systems. A rather tall stone building, the Tesla Science Center wouldn't look out of place in an old black-and-white monster flick. The guys found it rather easily after having carefully made sure to check and double-check their campus map before venturing out!

"Seriously, don't even worry about it. I'm sure no one noticed that the power went out for a tiny bit last night," August reassured Grant quietly, so that no one might have overheard them.

"A tiny bit!! It was knocked out for over three hours!!! I would die if anyone knew it was me who triggered it," exclaimed Grant, half into his shirt to muffle the sound.

"Relax, I'm telling you, no one even noticed. Everyone probably went to bed super early after a long first day of classes. Don't worry!" August assured him.

Opening the main doors, they sprinted into the building to make certain that they didn't add 'late to science class' to their list of accolades from the start of school at Blackstone Academy.

Heading down the hallway to their science class, they found themselves walking behind two of their fellow first-year classmates. It was Kasia from their history class the day before, and she was talking with her friend, Penelope.

"You noticed it too!" said Penelope.

"Argggh!!! Yes!! I had just finished my entire assignment, and was revising it one more time… when the power went out, and I was left sitting there in the dark, panicking," said Kasia.

"Oh, no! That's terrible, did you lose what you were working on?" replied Penelope.

"Wiped out my entire evening's worth of work. I had to stay up half the night to re-do it all before class today," said Kasia sleepily.

Hearing the news, Grant slowed his pace down the hall, wide-eyed with self-doubt. Taking a big gulp, he hoped to anything that Kasia didn't turn around, as at that moment his face would have given away everything.

"Such a nightmare, I wonder if we should go to the library to do our studying and homework from now on? Especially if this sort of thing keeps happening," questioned Penelope.

"Sigh, maybe. Otherwise, I might not get any sleep all semester, and end up a zombie!" said Kasia, the dark circles under her eyes highlighting the concern.

"Haha, no, no, no, we can't let that happen. I'd meet up with you to study today after classes, but I have tennis practice. What about later on?" asked Penelope.

"I have singing lessons until six. How about we meet in the library after then?" said Kasia.

The two girls rounded the corner of the hallway and entered the lab science classroom ahead of the guys. Grant stopped short and stared off into the distance, like a malfunctioning robot. Noticing that his friend had frozen in his tracks, August stopped too.

"So much for no one noticing. This sucks..." mumbled Grant under his breath.

"Well..." said August, as he passively ran his hands through his hair, not knowing what else to say.

At that moment, Headmaster Humboldt walked up beside them, as if right on cue!

"Well, what? You two lost your way again, so soon? This is becoming a regular habit of yours. Wonder if you two might not be lost causes, hmm," barked Headmaster Humboldt.

"We're not lost this time, sir. Our class is right over there, in fact," said August, as he pointed to the door of the science lab that the two girls had entered moments earlier.

"And yet you are standing here, with what is becoming an ever more familiar blank expression on your faces. Not sure I'd have recognized you otherwise," joked Headmaster Humboldt.

Looking from one of their faces to the other, Headmaster Humboldt realized that he was going to need to dig a bit deeper into his motivational repertoire, as it was clear that these weren't typical cases.

"Now, remember, you're never as far away from where you think you're going as when you admit defeat.

So, knock off the slouching routine, walk the extra five feet to the door, open it, and see if you can't make something of yourselves," he said.

Humboldt, continuing to pick up steam, rumbled on down the hallway, searching for other opportunities to compel students on to new scholarly heights. Whether they wanted the advice or not!

Inside the lab, a heated debate was kicking off between Shelby and a group of other students regarding the massive illustrative shortcomings of model volcanoes versus the value of firsthand field experience with their real-world counterparts.

Hearing the din, and fearing Shelby might end up going head first into a bucket of baking soda and vinegar, or be unceremoniously introduced to what a pants-load full of oatmeal lava felt like, August and Grant rushed to their neighbor's aid.

CHAPTER SEVEN

Outside Providence's premiere art museum, a large truck braved the sharp right-hand turn off North Main Street, into the shelter of the museum's property. Ever so carefully, calculating each move, the driver skillfully used his mirrors to bring the truck in, while protecting the precious cargo it held. Sitting beside him in the cab was a representative from the insurance underwriter, who was a man as straight-laced as his mustache.

From the loading dock, directing the entire operation was the ever-fastidious museum curator, who was waving and shouting directions to the truck driver like a mad conductor. Backing into the correct spot, the driver finally put the diesel engine into park. He breathed a loud sigh of relief, as he had reached his destination with not so much as a scratch on the bumper of the truck. With his window rolled down, the voice of the curator giving orders to the team of workers standing by to unload the truck could clearly be heard.

"Be extremely careful unloading each and every piece!! This is one of the finest collections we've ever had on loan here at the museum, and I intend to keep our spotless reputation intact!" yelled the curator.

Stepping out of the cab and approaching the museum curator, the representative from the insurance company had his attaché case in hand with all the prerequisite transfer documents prepared. Spotting him, the curator paused long enough from shouting at people to address the man civilly.

"Welcome, welcome! Are all the pieces here?" asked the curator.

Wiping his jacket sleeve across his mustache, the insurance agent said in a muffled voice, "Yes, all the pieces are accounted for. Here is the shipping manifest. Every single detail is precisely as we discussed on the phone."

"Excellent. It's such an honor to be displaying these masterworks in our gallery here!! We're intensely excited for the opening!" beamed the curator.

"I'm sure," answered the insurance agent dryly, as he looked like he was ready to sneeze or turn his nose up in the curator's general direction. Opening his attaché case, he gathered up the documents he required to be signed, making it obvious that he had no patience for trivial joviality.

Today, being a particularly strong example, as he found himself short on patience to an extreme. Having spent the prior twenty-four hours either trapped in the cramped quarters of the truck cab driving up from Philadelphia, or suffering with a bad back on a rigid uncomfortable spring mattress in the cheap hotel that the insurance company put him up in. His attitude did little to hide the fact that he despised aimless chit-chat, and he intended to get back on the road as soon as possible.

"Now, I'm going to need you to sign, here, here, and here," said the insurance agent, gesturing to the top-most document.

Taking up the outstretched pen, the curator was still elated at the prospect of having this entire traveling exhibit of real Titian works on display in his museum. It was practically a dream come true for this lifelong Renaissance art devotee. With the papers signed, the agent turned and gave a forced half-smile before getting right back into the truck, quarantining himself from any further social interaction.

His attention back on the workers unloading the truck, the curator barked some more orders.

"Any slip-ups, even the slightest hair out of line with these works, and you will not only be losing your jobs, but I will be making borscht this week with a very secret ingredient!" he shouted. Under his watchful eye, the crew continued to work, knowing that any false move would result in the verbal brow-beating of a lifetime.

Opposite the museum, across Waterman Street to the north, was the green surrounding Providence's First Baptist Church. Dotted with trees, the green was a well-manicured space within the city that helped define the line between College Hill and Downtown. Staying out of sight under the shade of a tree, and watching the entire scene unfold was another finely tailored man in a black suit. Eyes concealed momentarily behind sharp designer sunglasses, he took out a pair of binoculars that were hidden under his coat. Surveying the scene with intense interest, he settled his sights on the boxes being unloaded from the delivery truck.

"It's arrived. They're unloading all of the Titians now," said the mysterious man into his cell phone, which he struggled not to drop, as his hands were full. Listening

to the response on the other end of the line, he adjusted his grip on the binoculars, nearly fumbling them in the process. On his left hand, a crescent shaped scar was clearly visible as he leaned in closer to get a better look at the loading dock.

"I've counted only four thus far; they are being extremely careful with each one. 'You know who' is running the show, it's a painstakingly slow process with everything being handled with kid gloves. Haha, yeah, I know! He's inside going over the floor plan."

Inside the museum, it was like any other typical Thursday afternoon, empty floors, while all the walls are covered with tremendous works of art. The different collections held in a silence, broken only by the pitter-patter of intellectual types' footsteps and the occasional hushed conversation. Walking the gallery halls, another equally well-dressed and suspicious-looking gentleman was appreciating the establishment at his own pace. With the precision of an art appraiser, he was making notes of a different kind than all the other patrons. Mental notes, specifically of the layout of the museum's floor plan. He identified the locations of entrances, exits, security cameras, motion detectors and the spots favored by museum employees.

Slowing, as a museum docent walked past him,

the man stopped and flashed a brilliant, toothy grin at the docent before he continued on unassumingly. His hands held thoughtfully up to his face, eyes constantly shifting from target to target, he resumed his search. Pulling up his sleeve, he checked the time on his expensive watch. It was shortly after two o'clock.

***

Sitting at his desk in the back of Mr. Eastley's history classroom, with his head pressed into his arm, August was craving some exercise and excitement. Glancing up at the ticking clock on the wall above the blackboard, he could see that it was shortly after two o'clock. Last class of the day, and the minutes were dragging by. Mr. Eastley was getting close to finishing up his lecture; 'it won't be long now', August told himself, only a few more minutes...

"And that was the last time I went swimming in the Nile River, and for good reason too! It was surprisingly cold for that time of year, strange, really. But what else do we know about the Nile River?" asked Mr. Eastley, looking out over his classroom, surveying the landscape in search of raised hands.

Most of the students remained motionless, totally

zonked after such an academically demanding day. Only one hand in the entire classroom had gone up in response to Mr. Eastley's question. Pointing to the student, he called upon her.

"Kasia, yes?" said Mr. Eastley. She was quick to respond with an air of rehearsed confidence.

"That, unlike, say, the Mississippi River, the Nile River flows from south to north," said Kasia.

"Absolutely correct! Not only that, but it has some tremendously high falls in it. I sure learned that one the hard way! Yikes! Which gets me back to what I was saying earlier about the 'Patient Tales of Peter Whales'," said Mr. Eastley, absorbed in his own story.

August stirred at his desk, only two minutes left of class, and he can feel the life returning to him as the countdown progressed!

"Terribly brash fellow, this man Peter Whales. It wasn't until he came down with every possible illness imaginable, from chicken pox to sinusitis, and had to be holed up in a hospital for months on end, that he did indeed learn patience," rambled Mr. Eastley.

With that, the school bells chimed in the clock tower on the quad, marking the end of classes for the day. Dismissed, all the students flipped closed their texts and gathered up their things.

"Until next time then, everyone," called out Mr. Eastley.

Exiting the classroom, August caught up with Grant, as many other students rushed by them in the excitement of the end of another day of classes.

"Grant, you up for an excursion?" asked August.

"Where to?" followed Grant as they continued walking with the rest of the herd of students.

"Was told about this Asian restaurant on Hope Street that is supposed to be the best in the city; you interested?" mentioned August.

His stomach already rumbling audibly, Grant was instantly enthusiastic.

"Just point the way!"

CHAPTER EIGHT

High atop the rocky bluffs of Newport, RI, overlooking the water, were some of the most prized properties on the East Coast. Standing alone on the large, finely manicured grounds of one such Ocean Avenue address was Lexi Donovan. Her cell phone conversation was distracting her attention from her clients, who were admiring the details of the house's luxurious construction and stonework, pointing out to each other features that the home had to offer, and making plans for what they would like to see done to the property.

Lexi looked out towards the stretch of ocean before her. The sun was beginning to set, and the view out across the water was amazingly gorgeous. The sound of the crashing waves against the rocky coastline rolled over the property, bringing with it, both a sense of calm and imagination. Along with that feeling of awe in nature, that only someone who has seen the ocean can quite ever understand.

"Finishing up here now. The showing went very well. By the way, they are eating up the view. We should be in my office talking a firm offer tomorrow. A little hand-holding, a couple signatures, and it'll be time to crack open the champagne," said Lexi. Shifting her stance and turning away from the house, you could tell more important matters than real estate were on Lexi's mind.

"About that OTHER matter, all the details are taking shape. Yes, I know. It's a thing of beauty! I have everything worked out with a precision that would make Da Vinci jealous," laughed Lexi. "No, it won't be long now."

From the long circular driveway of the manor house, the prospective buyers waved to Lexi, trying to get her attention.

"Think I have my answer here, I'll talk to you later, oh I know!! Bye!" she said.

Tucking away her cell phone, and stashing it

safely in her bag, she headed back across the immense lawn up toward the house to discover whether her clients were seriously thinking about making an offer, or if it was going to require showing them yet another dozen properties!

Ocean Drive in Newport rarely disappointed, and Lexi had a strong feeling that this place would be the one. She always trusted her instincts, that was how she had become so successful in business, and she didn't intend for her luck to run out, not now, not ever.

***

Back in Providence on the East Side, leaving their bicycles on the sidewalk, Grant and August were poised in front of what they had been told was the home of the best Asian food in the city, an opinion further substantiated by a popular Rhode Island lifestyle and entertainment magazine. The unassuming exterior of the restaurant didn't speak nearly as loudly to the boys as the delicious smells wafting out from the kitchen.

Grant opened the door, already wanting to try everything on the menu! Inside, the inviting space had booths lining the walls, and a small reception stand in the back corner. All the dining tables on the main floor were

quite full, with a host of people grabbing an early dinner. Large paintings of Cambodian temples mirrored each other on either wall, and invited further exploration.

Finding an empty booth along the restaurant's far wall, August and Grant placed their orders after breaking through an intense bout of indecision over the glut of choices on the menu! Minutes later, each was happily eating in the type of silence brought about by really good food!

"This fried rice is excellent. Always have to try it whenever I go to a new place. It's tradition, and this one easily passes the test. But wow, this nime chow is as good as my favorite place back home in DC!" exclaimed Grant, as he grabbed another roll and doused it with delicious homemade peanut sauce.

On the other side of the table, August's face was all red from the really hot dish that he was eating. Still, it was clear from the big smile on his face that he was enjoying the righteous flavor from such a spicy dish!

"Haha, yeah, this place really holds up its end of the bargain. When they say spicy satay noodles, they mean SPICY! Great new dish to try, as it sure brings the heat. Could you pass me the water before my throat goes up in flames?!" August said, while waving his hands over his mouth, as if he was breathing fire.

Quickly, Grant passed the water over to August, who downed a glass of it in about two seconds. At the other end of the restaurant, by the entrance, two other Blackstone Academy students had walked in and were in search of empty seats.

"Look over there, isn't that Braylon Lee from school?" asked Grant, his mouth full of stir fry.

Confused, August asked "Who?" while he stared at the new arrivals trying to place them in his mind.

"Braylon Lee, he's a sophomore at the academy and from Hong Kong, originally. I met him at the Martial Arts club's first meeting. Guy is ridiculously good at Kung Fu, been training since he was four years old," said Grant.

"And the girl? She looks familiar, isn't she in our math class?" wondered August.

"That's Chloe, yeah, she is. Let's invite them over," said Grant.

Before August could answer, Grant was already up and motioning to their fellow students, who were talking with the hostess across the room.

"Braylon, Chloe, how's it going?! Why don't you come over here and join us, we've got room!" called out Grant.

Recognizing Grant, they both waved back at him,

Braylon with a big smile on his face, and Chloe a little more reserved. Crossing the room, they shuffled over to the booth where August and Grant had established themselves.

"Wondered how long it would take you to discover this place!" joked Braylon.

"Guess you guys had the same idea we did," added Chloe.

"The food is incredible. Here, let me push over and make some room," said Grant, getting up and sliding down closer to the wall.

Chloe and Braylon sat down in the booth opposite each other. The server brought them each menus, and they were already perusing their options.

"Guys, this is my roommate, August. August, this is Braylon and Chloe," said Grant, kicking off the introductions.

"Pleasure to have your acquaintance, we're in math class together, no?" said Chloe warmly, in her Scandinavian accent.

Nodding in response, August slightly blushed and smiled back. Braylon extended his hand to August from across the table to shake hands.

"Good to meet you," he said, with a friendly toothy grin.

"Likewise; Grant was just telling me you practice Kung Fu, Braylon, is that right?" asked August.

"Yeah, you should come to the next class. Check it out. Learn some wushu," said Braylon, as he made some elaborate hand movements in the air.

"Will do. Definitely count me in!" answered August enthusiastically.

"I can picture all three of you training, just like in the movies. With the inspirational music and everything, haha. All you need now is a villain and the picture is complete!" teased Chloe.

"Oh yeah, that's us alright, haha. Maybe Braylon here, but August and I? Eh, not so much!" said Grant, half sarcastically.

August continued to eat his noodles, and paused long enough to put out the freshly spreading heat in his mouth from the spices in the food, to add to the conversation.

"I still love the idea of having theme music, who wouldn't want that? Haha. Can't have a good montage without it, if only I were musically talented..." said August wistfully.

"I'll tell you who is musically talented, those four guys at lunch today who were having that baked-bean-eating contest. Oh, my god, I've never laughed so hard in my life," said Grant, recalling the events.

"Dang! How did I miss that?! This is a tragedy," exclaimed Braylon.

"More like good fortune, you could have been scarred for life and never able to eat legumes again!" prodded Chloe, with a wide grin on her face.

"Guess there's our answer, we hire those guys to produce, haha," chuckled August.

"Not on your life! You guys are too much! I'll never understand boys and their farts!" responded Chloe.

With that, the four new-found friends continued laughing and having a great time over delicious food at possibly the finest Asian restaurant in the city (the debate raged on!).

***

Darkness had fallen on the city, the entire skyline lit up by lights, as the energy of a Friday night had begun to take hold. August and his friends were far from the only ones out on an evening such as this. The upscale restaurants along Providence's waterfront were teeming with people. By the waterfront lagoon, a waiter carrying drinks navigated the active dining room of one such fine eatery. Working his way out from the noisy bar and through a set of ornate glass doors, he entered the patio area overlooking the dark fire-lit water.

At the corner table on the patio, the glow of the city lights cast soft shadows over the sharp outlines of the hardened faces of four men. Dressed all in black, one could easily wonder if they just left a funeral (or were ready for one). Reading the situation, the veteran waiter cautiously set down the next round of drinks on the table, and disappeared as quietly as he arrived.

Of the four men, two sat motionless, looking solemnly at their drinks, acting more as if they were in a trance than out for a night on the town, while the third man sipped his drink slowly, and was patiently watching the night sky. Leaned back in his chair, the last, and most dangerous looking man, was on the phone.

"All your orders are being carried out, with every detail accounted for. Just as we discussed, our ETA will be twelve-twenty," said the well-tailored man.

He paused, listening intently as he folded his napkin into smaller and smaller squares. Occasionally, he nodded in silent agreement and understanding.

"Been following all of the weather reports and everything matches up. We're going to drop in on our 'friends' first thing in the morning and make the switch. I'm looking forward to that, personally. A little karmic retribution there, haha, serves them right, I say!"

"Yeah, everything is mapped out, as well as the contingency route you wanted. We'll be ready and waiting for your cue. It's going to be a thing of beauty." The man laughed while no one else at the table seemed even the least bit amused.

"That's right, I'll tell everyone, and I can already feel my pulse quickening. The time has nearly come to make our mark."

Overhead, clouds were beginning to roll in from the northwest. A storm was coming.

"Good," was all he said, as he ended the call and reached for his drink.

Unwilling to be the first to speak and break the silence, everyone else at the table remained silent.

"Ah, my friends, we're mere hours away at this point. It's on us to deliver our end of the bargain if we're going to reach our payday," announced the man, as he turned his attention to his dinner companions.

Around the table, everyone seemed steady in their resolve.

"Vasal, no last minute changes I assume, we are all committed to the cause," said one of the other men.

For, within them all, momentum was building in their very hearts and minds. Perhaps even a tiny bit of

nervousness, too, for what they were soon intending to carry out.

Glasses raised, the crescent scar on his hand in clear display, Vasal called for a toast from his men.

"To the best of times, and most brilliant of crimes," he said, in a low but clear voice.

Everyone nodded, clashed glasses, and downed their drinks.

In the moonlight, even the most stubborn and pessimistic of passersby would have agreed, it really was a hauntingly beautiful late summer night in the city. The sounds of conversations, glasses striking, dinner plates rattling, and laughter from the restaurant, reached up into the darkness. All was well within the city tonight.

CHAPTER NINE

The rising sun across the Blackstone Academy campus cast the most wonderful rays of bright yellow, white, and gold sunshine on the steps of the freshman dorm. Sitting there by themselves were two students, looking at a magazine together, and talking softly.

Out for his usual morning bike ride, Headmaster Humboldt had already spotted the two girls sitting there aimlessly, in his eyes at least.

"Okay, what's going on here? Taking the day off from studying and all of your academic pursuits, I see," announced Headmaster Humboldt as he approached.

Looking very confused, the two girls froze in

shock. Meekly, they responded to the headmaster.

"But, sir, it's Saturday??" they squeaked out in unison.

"Weakest excuse I've ever heard for not thinking. Do yourselves a favor. Stop being apologists and apply yourselves! The world rewards hard work, and I expect great things from you," rattled on Humboldt.

Still baffled, the students sat there in awe of Headmaster Humboldt's presence.

"Y-y-yes, sir," they said.

"Alright then, don't just sit there, mouths gaping. Opportunity awaits!" said Humboldt, convinced that his words were sage advice.

Without waiting for a lucid response, Headmaster Humboldt pedaled off along the quad walkway, leaving the students to scramble and figure out how to apply themselves for the rest of their morning, while still not entirely sure whether they were coming or going!

Four floors up from that conversation, August was showing signs that he may imminently be stirring and possibly even getting up, his eyes half blinking, nose twitching.

Leaning to look out the window, August saw Headmaster Humboldt zipping around the sidewalks on the other side of the quad making his morning rounds.

Sharing with other students his unique brand of encouragement and feedback as he went, he made August feel somewhat relieved that neither he nor Grant were officially up yet, which, he acknowledged, of course, was also clear weekend tradition as he slumped back down into bed!

"You awake?" inquired August, his face hidden, half buried in a pillow.

"Nope, still dreaming about chive dumplings from the restaurant last night. They seriously changed my life. I'm a new man," said Grant, his voice muffled under a mound of blankets.

"As a new man, what do you feel like doing today? Weather looks flawless out there," coaxed August.

"It often is this time of year. And me? Nothing! I'm going to sleep all day, it's a professional decision," answered Grant, who was not budging.

Being the sort that required fresh air and regular activity to function, August got up out of bed. He looked out the window to confirm that yes, the day was indeed perfect, and not waiting for them.

"Don't blame you. It is a Saturday morning tradition after all," said August.

"Yes, indeed, and I am not one to dodge time-tested ceremony," said Grant, not wanting to upset his comfortable pile of blankets.

"Haha, that's too bad," replied August, drawing out his words in dramatic fashion, as if he were holding back a grand secret.

Finally, August had managed to grab the smallest foothold of his roommate's attention, as Grant turned over and showed some sign of alertness.

"How's that?" said Grant, with only the slightest interest.

"'Cause they are serving all-you-can-eat waffles in the commissary until eleven o'clock. Supposed to be incredible... Fluffy waffles, golden maple syrup..." said August.

Flipping off the covers and grabbing up his stuff, Grant quickly motored into action.

"Alright, alright, I'm up!!" shouted Grant, now clearly convinced.

The two friends laughed as they headed out the door, stomachs rumbling, in the pursuit of the breakfast delight that was waffles.

The awesomeness of Blackstone Academy's Saturday morning waffle extravaganza was the worst kept secret on campus, as nearly all the students turned out early to enjoy them! It was comical to see so many students up early (relatively speaking, as it was after ten o'clock by this point!) on a Saturday morning. Very few of them could match August or Grant's appetite for waffles. With each roommate finishing off a monster stack, both August and Grant laid down their forks and pushed the maple syrup container away from their side of the table.

"I'm done, can't eat anymore," groaned Grant, clutching his sides.

"Ugh, I've never been this full in my life. I might need an organ transplant at this point, no joke," croaked August from his chair next to Grant at the table.

Sitting across from them was Kasia, and her best friend, Penelope. Taking a completely opposite approach to breakfast, they were each enjoying one waffle and delicately cutting it into small cube-shaped pieces before slowly chewing and eating it proper-like.

Penelope couldn't help but giggle as she put down her glass of orange juice and watched the two boys groaning and holding their stomachs.

"Very impressive, how many was that for each of you? Could have sworn I saw you go up there at least three times for seconds. Although can you really call them seconds if they are thirds and fourths??" she said.

August and Grant took their sweet time to reply,

as they didn't want to upset the very delicate digestive balancing act currently churning in their stomachs.

"Must have been seven for me. I think I'm going blind in one eye from too much maple syrup goodness," said August, with a long sigh.

Not speaking, Grant merely held up eight fingers.

"Eight, wow, I hope you weren't planning on moving for the rest of the day, haha," giggled Penelope.

"I have a feeling these two weren't planning on anything, like the fact that their blood sugar is about to go through the roof!" chimed in Kasia.

Gulping, August and Grant had sad looks on their faces.

"Uh, actually, we were sorta planning on heading downtown later this afternoon to do some exploring; want to come?" added August, while trying to force himself to drink some water.

Unaware that August was going to extend the girls an invitation, Grant turned a bright shade of red, and held his breath, waiting for their response.

Under the table, he kicked August, who fired back at him a look of bewilderment as to the root of this undercover shin-hitting outburst. Penelope was the first to answer.

"I have tennis practice at four, but I'm free until

then. What do you think Kasia?"

"Sure, we can meet you at Waterplace Park, say, one o'clock?" said Kasia.

Showing signs of life from the guys' side of the table, August perked up.

"One o'clock, yeah, that'd be great."

"If you guys can make it of course. Your friend is looking a little green there," said Kasia, motioning over towards Grant.

"Oh, him? He's fine... I think... might just need a glass of water or something to right the ship is all," said August, feigning confidence.

Poor Grant made a whimpering noise, as he couldn't believe the turn of events that was unfolding, and what he was hearing.

"Hope so. Well, we're heading back over to the dorms, but we'll be sure to meet you in the park. Wave if you see us," said Kasia.

"You got it, see you then!" said August.

"Bye," called out Penelope.

Picking up their plates, the girls walked off and soon disappeared into the crowd of students leaving the cafeteria. Waving, the guys breathed a sigh of relief. By now the place had pretty much emptied out, save a few stragglers like August and Grant.

"Hangout this afternoon? Whatever possessed you to invite them?!?!" demanded Grant.

"I don't know, they just seemed nice," stumbled August, as he tried to search for the right words to diffuse the situation, as Grant was visibly annoyed.

"And they said yes, I mean, they said yes, do you really think they'll be there??" wondered Grant aloud.

"Would be nice, either way though, we can still keep our plans to explore," replied August.

"Man, I can't believe you sometimes, you know that? Totally out of left field with this stuff, haha. But I'm glad you did ask, and you're right, they do seem cool," announced Grant, who was becoming more and more comfortable with the idea by the second.

Getting up, the two of them brought over the teetering mountain of dishes that they'd generated over the course of the last hour, to be cleaned. While walking, August spotted a pair of glasses, as well as a magazine without an owner, left over on a table by the windows.

"Hey, don't those look like Professor Eastley's glasses?" noted August.

"Maybe, can't tell from here," said Grant.

Curious, August instinctively decided to go over and investigate. He glanced around the cafeteria, but it was now devoid of people to ask about them.

"Must be, Grant, look, it's an article on Ancient Mesopotamia," said August, flipping through the open magazine.

Convinced, they picked up the pair of glasses, and snagged the magazine, before leaving the cafeteria. Both of the guys were blissfully unaware that things weren't quite as simple as they might first appear.

CHAPTER TEN

Blackstone Blvd. and the East Side of Providence were home to many beautiful and stately properties. Tudors, Mediterranean homes, Federal, Greek Revival, they were all there. A squirrel, taking a flying leap from a branch, landed safely amongst the canopy of leaves on precisely one such architecturally enriched, tree-lined street.

On the walkway below, the squirrel mistrustfully eyed a duo of contractors leaving the nearby three-story house that they had recently completed work on. The two contractors, brothers, both with unkempt hair hidden under stained baseball caps, couldn't help but gloat as they shuffled back towards the street, waiting until they were out of earshot of the residence before they began talking.

"Ah, I love it, the payment is all here, can you believe it, Frankie?" said the taller one, who was wearing a particularly greasy tank top that looked like it hadn't been washed, ever.

Chuckling, his portly companion wiped his runny nose on his left sleeve and adjusted his jeans, which seemed to be covering much less of his rump than everyone would agree should be allowed by common decency.

"I know! It's awesome! We quadrupled our price estimate, double-charged for hours, sub-contracted the work out to a guy who didn't know what he was doing, and they STILL had to pay us! Obviously, one of your most brilliant ideas ever, Billy"

"Suckers! If only they gave out trophies for ripping people off, I'd need to build another basement to hold them all!" said Billy, clearly proud of himself.

"All in a day's work. I was also thinking we could add an extra week of fees onto the Jansen account, milk that a bit, too," said Frankie, his equally suspect and morally corrupt partner.

"You mean the seventy-year-old widow who we are painting the kitchen for?" asked Billy.

The two crooked contractors crossed the street, heading over to their van that was parked down the block. The rusty and crusty beat up van stood out, with 'Butternut Painting' written on either side in large letters.

"That's the one," confirmed Frankie.

"Haha, the senile old bag will never know the difference. Yeah, let's do it. Good work!" chuckled Billy as he scratched a rash on the side of his neck.

Approaching the van, neither of them noticed the two 'gentlemen' dressed in all black, waiting for them on the opposite side of the van. The men were patiently poised for one of the contractors to simply reach out a hand and open the passenger side door. Then they would spring into action against their unsuspecting prey!

Completely clueless, Billy walked around to the driver's side, ignorant that there was anything out of the ordinary, or of what karma had coming to him. At the same time, Frankie rolled left to the van's large sliding door.

A quick strike to the back of Frankie's head landed simultaneously as he opened the rusted sliding door. It was enough to knock him senseless, as his seemingly invisible assailant unceremoniously dumped his body into the back of the van, and slammed the door shut behind him.

Making the turn around the front of the vehicle, Billy came face-to-face with the second taller gentlemen dressed in black.

"Uh, wha?" mumbled a startled Billy, his eyes fixed on the crescent-shaped scar on the man's hand. The only response he received was the man in black grabbing him roughly, and slamming him against the side of the van hard enough to make his teeth rattle.

With a handgun pressed up under his chin, and his arm pinned behind his back, Billy couldn't move an inch.

"I need to borrow your keys, if you don't mind," said Vasal forcefully to Billy.

Seconds later, the van casually pulled out from the quiet street, using its blinker as it made a proper U-turn to head towards Downtown Providence, with the tall man dressed in black behind the wheel.

***

Exiting the cafeteria, Grant stretched and let out a big yawn, as he and August traipsed down the front steps of the building. Blue skies awaited them, as it was a wonderful day outside. The exact sort that was meant for exploring!

"Should we maybe stop by Professor Eastley's classroom and drop off these glasses for him?" asked Grant.

"Was thinking that too, but then I remembered, on Friday in class he said he was going to be working over at the art museum today, so we could totally swing by there before meeting up with Penelope and Kasia. Plus, it's even on our way," pointed out August.

"That's right, that does kinda ring a bell. Okay, yeah, let's do that, then. Have you been to the museum before? I remember seeing a poster for it, advertising a new exhibit going up or something," agreed Grant.

"Haven't been, no, but I know where it is. Should be able to find the professor there, no problem," said August.

In the distance, Grant spotted the outline of a very familiar cyclist heading in their general direction. He stopped short, and grabbed August's arm.

"Uh, seems we're about to have some company, and a healthy dose of 'constructive' criticism," said Grant, his eyes focused about an odd fifty yards or so ahead of them.

"You know, I was kind of thinking a scenic route around campus might not be a bad idea. Since it's such a nice day out," said August, his eyes also trained on the swiftly approaching cyclist.

"Good point! Is a nice day out, and I'm always up for a little extra exercise," added Grant.

Making an abrupt right turn, the two boys alertly crossed the campus green and made for the athletic fields. Utilizing this roundabout way to get past the dorms, they hurried onward. Behind them, the familiar shadow of Headmaster Humboldt zipped across the walkway and on towards the cafeteria building.

CHAPTER ELEVEN

On the outskirts of campus, beyond the shadow of the large Leonidas Center gymnasium, were the school's four tennis courts. Surrounded by tall twelve-foot-high chain link fences, the courts had seen more than a few drag-out battles over the years. A bunch of students were making good use of the courts right now and playing some competitive matches.

A particularly riveting contest was finishing up on the court at the end of the complex. Serving, the girl called out the score count.

"Advantage in!" yelled Chloe, her long blonde hair tied up in a ponytail.

On the other side of the net, Braylon waited for the serve, mind focused, body relaxed, not unlike his preparation for a martial arts sparing session. Spinning his racket, he prepared himself to launch into action, knowing this could be the last play of the game!

Ready, Chloe lofted the ball up into the air and powered through her serve. With fantastic speed, the tennis ball shot over the net where it bounced once before being met with Braylon's racket, as he sprinted to his right.

Sending the ball back and forth, time after time, Braylon ran around the court faster and faster, as neither player was willing to surrender the match! Backhands, jarring near-dives for the ball, lobs, spinning shots, the volley continued on and on! Working from the center, Chloe plotted each and every move, sending Braylon all the way to the left of the court, only to have him make a brilliant play, just barely keeping the ball in bounds and the game alive.

Sensing her opponent was reeling, Chloe knew she had him right where she wanted him! Incorporating a swift backhand, she zoomed the ball over the net towards the opposite right-hand corner of the court. Seeing the cross-court play in motion, Braylon tried valiantly to get back into position. But alas, he was too late, his feet in a veritable tangle, trying to move as fast as his mind was urging them to. Reflexes lost in the shuffle, he stumbled, the streaking ball landing in bounds, only centimeters beyond the reach of his outstretched racket.

Game, set, and match to Chloe! On her side of the net she was already celebrating her victory in style. Braylon stopped and looked at his racket as if he half expected to see an actual hole in it that the ball had somehow slipped through. Turning, he smiled and walked over to meet Chloe, who was taking a drink from her water bottle. Braylon knelt down and grabbed up his own water bottle.

"Good game! I guess you weren't kidding when you said I'd be running today! I was all over the place, left, right, backwards, and upside down practically!" laughed Braylon, as he drummed on the back of his head with his racket.

Smiling, Chloe set down her water bottle and checked the text messages on her phone.

"Thanks, I had to try something to keep up with you," she joked.

"Well, you sure did that, and THEN some. And clearly, now it's me who should be the one getting some lessons, haha," said Braylon.

"Couldn't hurt!" quipped Chloe with a smirk.

"What?!?!!!" roared Braylon, faking surprise.

Seeing Braylon recognize the dig she snuck into the conversation and the expression on his face, Chloe almost spilled her water laughing.

"Haha, I'm only teasing, you played great out there. Really! I like it best when both sides can win some games, and for the most part, keep things evenly matched and competitive," said Chloe, assuaging his ego.

"Me too, at the rate you are going, though, you'll be able to beat Winston in the school tournament!" he announced, clearly impressed.

"You think so? They say he is the best player at the academy. I heard about the matches he played last year when he won the title, and I can't imagine him not being able to win it again... Do you suppose his brother August can play as well as he does?" wondered Chloe.

"Hmm, good question. Let's ask him!" said Braylon.

"Huh??" replied Chloe. It now being her turn to act surprised, as she didn't realize that Winston was walking over to them as they had been talking!

Having finished his warm-up stretches, Winston was gearing up for a few matches himself, as he had reserved the court that they were finishing up on to play next.

"Winston! Hey, we were just talking about you! I met your younger brother, August, the other night. Guess he is following in your footsteps by coming to school here, eh?" said Braylon.

"That's right, he's probably holed up in the library right now, studying," said Winston.

"The library?? I don't think I've ever seen you go there before, Winston, haha," laughed Braylon.

"Get outta here! Hah. It's more that the city is totally different from the countryside, where we grew up. And if I know my brother, he's probably so completely overwhelmed by everything that he is keeping a very low profile," said Winston.

"That's funny, because I could swear that is him over there right now!" said Braylon, pointing towards two first-year students who were walking past the courts and heading off the Blackstone Academy campus grounds.

"No way, uh, wait a second, you're right, that is my brother!!" blurted out Winston.

"Hey! August!" he yelled loudly, trying to get his brother's attention.

Having identified his brother, Winston took off after him, leaving all his stuff on the court.

With Winston gone, Chloe and Braylon gathered

up the rest of their own gear and headed off towards the dorms.

"Seems like kind of a rather strange family, those Winters, don't you think?" whispered Chloe, in a very hushed tone, so that only Braylon could hear as they walked.

Shrugging his shoulders, Braylon pondered what would be a thoughtful response as he carefully assessed the situation first in his own mind.

"I'm sure we'll be learning a lot more about them both as school goes on. In the meantime, I'm much more concerned about your tennis game, as you were a tad bit slow out there today!" said Braylon.

And with that he took off running, leaving Chloe to digest his latest zinger!

"Slow?? Why, you!!!! Hey!!!!" yelled Chloe as she chased after him.

Beyond the sight of the tennis courts, westward running Angell Street was bustling with activity on this beautiful September afternoon. The sidewalks were full of foot traffic as people stopped in and out of their favorite coffee shops, and browsed in the local stores.

Winston finally caught up with August and Grant, who were waiting at a crosswalk for the light to change. All fully decked out in his tennis gear, the two

roommates looked a little bit surprised to see Winston, especially at this street corner, away from campus.

Winston was panting, having sprinted to catch up with the guys. Cars, and the occasional city bus, whizzed by behind them, as the traffic light remained green.

"Winston? What are you doing here?" wondered August aloud.

Still attempting to fully catch his breath, Winston was slow to answer.

"Saw you guys from the tennis courts. I tried to yell and get your attention. If I didn't know better, I would have thought you were trying to ditch me!" said Winston, wheezing ever so slightly.

"No, the only thing we're trying to avoid is yet another lecture from Headmaster Humboldt," responded Grant.

"Hahaha, I've been there! His 'pep talks' are legendary. Seriously though, you should take it as a compliment, as not everyone gets such a privilege," said Winston.

"But twice in one week? We don't want to be THAT popular or privileged!" pointed out August.

The streetlight turned red and the pedestrian crossing sign gave them the okay to proceed, so they all crossed over and followed the sidewalk ahead. Rambling along, they passed a solid handful of inviting-looking restaurants, including one with a giant fork displayed over the entrance that August made a mental note of to return to someday!

"As exciting as this walk to remember is, I really should get back and practice; don't want to lose my edge. Being so winded is already making me feel out of shape. Have a bunch of sweet new trick shots up my sleeve this year though, can't make things easy for the competition," said Winston.

"Darn right, no surrender!" chimed in Grant, as he offered up a strong high-five to Winston.

"Nice Y-chromosome moment going on here, very inspirational. I'll see you around campus, Winston," said August, with a hint of sarcasm, as he continued to walk on.

"Hey, wait! Your classes going alright? Feel like I should be asking all this stuff," said Winston, with a genuine look of interest on his face.

"Thanks, they are good. I like it so far, school, I mean," answered August, recognizing his older brother's sincerity.

"You guys stay out of trouble. I'm not always going to be there to keep an eye on you 24/7. Where are you going now, anyways??" asked Winston.

"We're going to an art museum, what could possibly go wrong?" returned August, as nonchalantly as humanly possible.

"Good point! That is certainly harmless enough. I'll see you guys later then!" said Winston, pointing at the two of them and signaling that he was watching their every move.

Completing a 180-degree turn, Winston jogged off back in the direction of the Blackstone Academy tennis courts.

"Later, Winston!" yelled Grant after him.

"See ya!" added August.

Winston acknowledged their comments with a series of fist pumps as he ran, soon disappearing out of sight. Once again, the glorious journey from campus to the art museum continued for August and Grant as they proceeded on foot!

CHAPTER TWELVE

The normally very quiet alley behind the art museum was filled with the sound of a rusted midsize van pulling up, breaking the tranquility of the space with its rumbling engine and hissing brakes. On both sides of the van, the words 'Butternut Painting' can be made out next to the picture of an actual butternut squash. Coming to a stop, the lone driver of the van jumped out of the cab, and with purpose walked up the steps to the loading dock platform and pounded on the service entrance door with his fist. Vasal was dressed in his usual black suit and wearing dark shades.

Noise from within the building confirmed that

someone inside had heeded the call. Slowly, the door opened with a grinding metallic clang as it revealed the weathered face of the loading dock manager, who looked at the stranger in front of him with a grumpy expression.

"What can I do for ya?" asked the loading dock manager in a gruff tone.

Turning his head slightly to the side, Vasal didn't say a word. Perplexed, the manager mimicked his action and tilted his head to the side accordingly, as if compelled to try and understand what the guy was trying to tell him through imitation.

Again, Vasal tilted his head even further to the side and stared blankly at the loading dock manager. Despite the warning in his head, the manager followed suit once more, looking like a dog when it jars its head to one side, as if to say, "I don't understand!"

At that moment Vasal struck, and with one punch knocked the manager flat out. He landed hard on the cement floor with a dull thud.

"Stop copying me," Vasal said with emphasis, to the unconscious man at his feet.

Stepping over the knocked out manager, as if he were some old luggage, Vasal signaled to the van that the coast was clear. He then emptied the fallen manager's pockets and grabbed the set of keys for the elevators and museum doors.

From the van, there was a flurry of movement as the back doors swung open. Three guys in black suits jumped out. The first turned back and prepared to close the door. Inside, the van was filled with paint supplies and random junk, though it was clear that some of it had been emptied out to make room for all the occupants. At the far end of the van, the two crooked contractors were tied up, with duct tape over their mouths. Seeing the light shining into the van, they squirmed and tried to make noise in protest.

Stifling a devious grin, the second man in black put his finger up to his mouth and took out a pistol from a holster under his jacket.

"Shhhhhh!" he whispered. Instantly, the pair of contractors froze and didn't make a peep.

Closing the van doors, the second man in black locked the van and pocketed the key. From around the corner, a silver luxury sports car sped onto the scene and parked right next to the painters' van. The third man in black rushed over to the car and opened the driver's side door.

Stepping out was a woman dressed in all black and wearing dramatic sunglasses. It was none other than Lexi Donovan, the real estate mogul! She was radiating with excitement as she exited the vehicle.

"Time for a little art appreciation! Oh, it's too exciting!" she said, unable to hide her perfectly white teeth as she smiled. Clearly delighted by the events in motion, Lexi was almost shivering.

Doubling back from the doorway of the loading dock, Vasal came with an update for Lexi, who, despite her disarming appearance, was here to run the show.

"Hope the guards are ready for a nice nap, as this sleeping gas is potent stuff! Shall we?" questioned Vasal, his mask in hand.

"Lead the way!" exclaimed Lexi, with a visible bounce in her step.

Before heading in, everyone put on ski masks to hide their faces. Picking up canisters that looked like miniature fire extinguishers, three of the four men entered the building followed by Lexi. The fourth stayed behind, as the van's getaway driver, and to keep an eye out for police interference.

Moving fast, the assembly of thieves made their way straight to the service elevator that leads up into the main portion of the museum. With his newly acquired keys in hand, Vasal had no difficulty bypassing the outer security system and entering the premises. It was clear that they knew just where they were going, having visited the museum, and studied the building's blueprints so thoroughly. One of the men was carrying several large duffel bags. The interior of the service elevator was huge and they all had no trouble fitting into it, with Lexi standing in the center, still giddy with excitement.

She extended a gloved hand and pressed the button for the fourth floor. After the doors slid shut, the elevator lurched into motion. Moments later, the sound of a chime announced their arrival. As the elevator rocked to a stop, the doors slid open simultaneously. Instantly, the band of thieves split up into three groups. One man remained at the elevator while the rest of the party rushed straight into the 19th Century American art exhibit, before heading off in different directions.

Turning left, Lexi froze in the doorway to the special exhibition. Doing a quick head count of everyone in the room, she started the stopwatch on her wrist with a countdown of 30 seconds.

Sprinting for the front reception desk, one of the men in black readied his canister of potent sleeping gas. Approaching the desk from behind, he flew up the short stairs, past the prominently displayed Contemporary Art exhibit, and sprayed the poor woman at the reception desk with sleeping gas, which immediately knocked her out cold.

Seizing the opportunity, he immediately locked the front doors. Pressing a button on his wristwatch, it blinked red, signaling to Lexi that his task was complete. The countdown on his wristwatch already stopped, with a generous reading of 14 seconds remaining!

"Clear!" growled the man into his watch's com-link system.

Vasal was storming down a flight of stairs on the third floor when he saw one of the lights on his watch flash red, while his own 30-second timer continued to countdown. Reaching the landing at the bottom, he burst through the door marked 'Security Control Room'.

Inside there wasn't a single soul in sight, just two empty black office chairs! Where could the guards be??! Glancing left and right frantically, he looked for any signs of activity… but there was nothing.

His pulse quickened. On the wall of monitors in front of him, he saw the other thieves in their positions around the museum! Beads of sweat began to form on his brow. Where were the guards??

From behind him, the unmistakable vwhooshing of a toilet's flush tore Vasal's attention away from the monitors. Towards the opposite end of the control room he spied a closed bathroom door. As the door handle turned, his heart rate increased, as well as his grip on the knockout gas canister.

Light spilled into the room; Vasal was now face-to-face with the 'missing' security guard. Neither could tell who was more surprised at seeing the other standing there at that moment!

"Uhhhhh…" coughed the stunned silhouette in a second of sheer, utter amazement, as normally this was such a sleepy and dull job for him.

It was Vasal who was first able to break out of the awkwardness-induced stupor that had captured both men. Raising his canister of sleeping gas, he pointed it at the poor guard.

"Very sorry about this mate, nothing personal!" he said apologetically, as he hit the trigger.

Instantly, the knockout gas went to work. Breathing in the fine mist, the security guard crumpled and dropped to the control room floor, where he was fast asleep. Vasal, checking his watch, discovered that the countdown timer had already lapsed and reached zero.

"Crap!" he yelled out, to no one in particular. Cursing his luck, he pressed the button on his watch all the same, causing a second light on the watch to turn red, signaling to his fellow thieves that his position within the museum was secured.

Seeing the last light on her watch turn red, Lexi

knew the building had been fully infiltrated by her hired operatives. Now they all could proceed with their plan!

Coming into Lexi's sight, Vasal and the other thief in black sprinted back to her position at the entrance to the Special Exhibits wing, which currently featured the works of the Renaissance master Titian.

"A feast for the eyes, such incredible work! Shows complete mastery of the medium," commented Lexi as she gazed at the beautiful works of art, as every wall was filled with works by the famous artist. The three thieves stood in the doorway in awe of the artistic presence that this space held.

***

Outside, turning off Benefit Street and passing the sign for the art museum, August and Grant walked down the ramp to the museum entrance. Reaching out for the large glass door, August tried to open it and was very surprised to discover that it was locked.

"That's weird… What time is it?" asked August.

"Can't be much past twelve-thirty. According to the hours listed here, it should still be open," answered Grant, looking perplexed.

The two peered in through the glass doors to see

if there was any activity inside. They could see the reception desk, but it was deserted. All the lights were on inside, but not a soul was in sight.

"Strange. Well I guess we can just hold onto Mr. Eastley's glasses for him, and give them back to him in class on Monday," said August.

"Fingers crossed that they're just reading glasses, haha. Otherwise, I'm hoping Mr. Eastley hasn't been attempting to drive without these! 'Cause I've seen how blind my mom is without hers, and it would be rather frightening to picture him behind the wheel," said Grant.

Being silly, Grant put the glasses on and blinked a few times as the lens magnified his eyes to twice their normal size. Somewhat amused, August laughed at him, and then looked once more through the window and knocked on the door a bit, making sure that there really wasn't any response from within.

"Well, we're getting nowhere fast. Monday it is, then," said August making a futile go at the door handle.

"It's nearing one o'clock, and time for our meet and greet. This is shaping up to be a really, really good day. Do you know the way?" asked Grant.

"Yeah, it's right around here, I believe. Let's hope we have better luck finding Waterplace Park than we did Mr. Eastley," answered August.

They turned back up the ramp to the street, leaving behind the museum that, by all appearances, looked vacant. Little did they realize that that couldn't have been further from the truth, as events within were unfolding at a rapid pace!

***

Back inside the Special Exhibits Gallery, Lexi and the finely tailored thieves were busying themselves working with surgeon-like precision. On the floor in the center of the room was one of the large duffel bags. Its contents were laid bare, which included a handful of canvas wraps, duct tape, rope and a few other odds and ends of the thievery trade. Around the room there were several visitors to the museum, who had clearly been given a dose of the knockout gas and were slumped over and sleeping peacefully. It was actually rather an odd sight, especially given the formality of the surroundings, like some art installation gone wrong!

Working together, the two thieves had followed Lexi's orders to the most exacting detail and taken down select pieces of art from the walls. Stealing a moment, Lexi ran her hands across the frame of one of the pieces of work that had caught her eye, before allowing the two men beside her to carefully extract it from the wall and hold it steady in front of her. "I can't get over it. And soon to be ours! Okay, package it up while I pick out the next one, time is running short," said Lexi.

All the commotion in the room had drawn some outside attention, as one of the volunteer art historians had entered the room. Even without his glasses, the recognizable face and presence of Mr. Eastley would have been easily identifiable to any of his students, had they been there. Unable to see that well, he squinted as he confronted the source of all the blasted noise!

"Excuse me! What is the meaning of all this ruckus?! Don't you know how to behave in a museum! Simply disgraceful!" boomed Mr. Eastley.

Not expecting any company, Lexi and the two thieves stopped cold in their tracks, setting down the painting they were carrying ever so gently. Not moving, they carefully considered how to proceed, looking from one to the other.

"What? Do you think if you don't move I can't see you! I'm not some dinosaur, I'll have you know, I was once awarded the Royal Norwegian Order of Merit by King Olav the fifth himself!" declared Mr. Eastley.

Slightly dumbfounded by the old fellow's bluster, the thieves stared blankly back at Mr. Eastley, seemingly mesmerized by his words. (Not unlike his students in first period class on a Monday morning!).

Coming to their aid was the extra member of their team, as he had slipped away from his post at the elevator. Sneaking up behind Mr. Eastley, he readied a blast of knockout gas for the old man. Hitting the trigger, he sprayed the fumes directly into Eastley's face in a big cloud of vapor. Mr. Eastley coughed loudly and gasped for air, as if he'd just inhaled the exhaust fumes from a double decker bus that had driven by.

"Ugh, what on Earth was that?? My word!" stammered and coughed Mr. Eastley.

Looking at the spray can he just used, and then back to Lexi, the thief realized it hadn't had quite the desired effect, yet. Both Lexi and Vasal were silently shaking their heads up and down, as if to say...

"Yeah, hit him again, you idiot!!"

Getting the message, he shook the canister up like it was whipped cream, before letting Mr. Eastley have it a second time in a gaseous flurry!!

"You know…oh, balderdash…" sputtered Mr. Eastley as he tried to speak, choking with every breath.

And like that, he fell back and was fast asleep on the gallery floor, completely dead to the world! Everyone in the room responded by returning to action, as that diversion had cut into their precious time for getting in and out of the museum.

"Great job! Now quickly get back and hold the elevator!" said Vasal. Taking that cue, the thief who had 'saved the day' didn't need to be asked twice this time, and left everyone else to finish up.

"Let's get this all cleared, only take what we can carry safely in hand. We need to load up the van and get ourselves out of here before we have any other even more 'educational' visitors!" ordered Lexi, with a firm determined look on her face.

"Good times! Sometimes you have to roll with the punches, and adapt to the unexpected, you know what I mean?" said Vasal.

"Yes, I sure do, but we've got what we came for," returned Lexi.

Heeding her words, they picked up the pace and finished wrapping in canvas the last of the paintings they intended to make vanish from the museum proper.

CHAPTER THIRTEEN

Having failed in their mission to deliver the glasses to Mr. Eastley, August and Grant headed down the rest of the hill to meet up with their friends at Waterplace Park. On the opposite side of the street from the guys stood the tall ornate spire of the oldest Baptist Church in America, founded by Roger Williams and built in 1774.

Relaxing on the grassy lawn, comfortably leaned up against a tree, there was a teenage boy sitting reading. Lost in the words before him, his heavy flannel shirt, jeans, and cowboy boots seemed a bit out of place for such a warm late-summer afternoon in the city. Parked next to him was an electric blue, eighteen-speed bicycle.

Yet that was not what caught the attention of August and Grant, as they were focused on their side of the street and the traffic at the intersection below.

"Check out this bus, it's heading straight for that wall?!?!" shouted Grant, his gaze directed at the busy streets at the bottom of the hill.

Directly in front of them, August now saw the public transit bus that was revving up its engine and switching into gear, as it picked up speed, heading toward the brick wall just out of their sight. Rushing over to see what was happening, the two friends came up against the railing overlooking the street beneath them and discovered it not to be a wall at all! Rather, it was the entrance to an underground tunnel into which the bus zoomed, making a loud swooshing sound as it went into the darkness, sending stray newspapers flying up into the air after it for dramatic effect.

"Well, that explains that, haha. I was practically bracing myself for the sound of the impact and then it's only a tunnel, ahhh!" cried Grant in relief.

Leaning over the railing, they spotted the tunnel's 'Do Not Enter' sign down at the street level.

"Wonder where it comes out?" asked Grant.

"Somewhere on the East Side or beyond I'd guess," said August, shrugging his shoulders.

Having stopped, they lingered for a moment on the spot. Looking up and down the adjoining alleyway, August caught sight of movement by the loading dock at the end of the alley. Peering closer, he made out the shape of several men in black suits wearing masks and carrying large items wrapped in canvas and loading them into the back of a van. Out of nowhere the distinct sound of a ringing alarm could be heard, causing the men in black to hasten their movements and bark unintelligible orders at one another.

Putting the pieces together in his head, August nudged Grant and gestured towards the van and loading dock. Seeing all the men in masks rushing out of the museum, they immediately knew something was up.

"What the...?!" said Grant.

"It's beginning to make sense why the museum door was locked..." answered August.

"Yeah! 'Cause the place is getting ripped off!! Either that or they are just rejects from some weird performance art skiing fashion exhibit. What should we do?! Call the cops?!!" suggested Grant.

"Definitely, just have to get to a payphone. See one anywhere?" asked August looking around, as neither he nor Grant carried a cell phone.

"No, nowhere, they are an endangered species it